To my loved ones,
Especially my husband, Kevin, who believes in me and in my dreams;
My parents, Rolly and Leny, and my sister, Ting, who support me unconditionally;
And my dog, Scotch, who brings so much joy into my life.
—M.L.C.

mascotbooks.com

With You

For more information, please contact:
Mascot Books
620 Herndon Parkway, Suite 320
Herndon, VA 20170
info@mascotbooks.com

Library of Congress Control Number: 2020908212

CPSIA Code: PRT1120A
ISBN-13: 978-1-64543-074-2

Printed in the United States

With You

Michelle Lopez Clark

Illustrated by Nidhom

With you I can do anything,

I don't feel so alone.

I can eat, read, and play all day,

Toss you a yummy bone.

With you I get excited,

I am as happy as can be.

I have a best friend in you,

You have a best friend in me!

With you my nights are sweeter,

I am not scared of the dark.

I can fight a dragon in my dreams,

Until you wake up and bark.

With you my days are brighter,

Even when I am sad.

You put a smile on my face,

Even when I am mad.

With you life's an adventure,

I am up for anything.

Your button nose and puppy eyes,

What love and joy you bring!

With you I get sweet kisses,

And fuzzy cuddles, too.

I'm proud to call you family,
oh, how much I love you!

From the Author

I wrote *With You* to encourage families to share more meaningful moments together. Valuing shared experiences with children, much like storytime, can help create a deeper and more loving relationship.

Storytime is more than just reading books with children. It is an opportunity to connect with them on an emotional level, and to nurture the bond they have with you. Sharing meaningful moments and conversations with children cultivates trust and a secure attachment style. Children who are securely attached with their caregivers are more likely to develop a strong and healthy sense of self.

After reading this book with your children, talk about the book and ask questions, such as:

- "What was the story about?"
- "What do you like about this book?"
- "Which dog in the story is your favorite?"

Share your own thoughts and feelings about the book as well, but don't stop there. Share with your children how you feel and what you experience when you are with them, much like the story. You could start by saying:

- "With you I feel..."
- "With you I can..."

With warmest wishes,
Michelle Lopez Clark

Michelle Lopez Clark is a Gottman Bringing Baby Home Educator and psychotherapist specializing in relationships, multicultural issues, and life transitions. She holds a master's degree in clinical mental health counseling from Marymount University and is an advocate for mental health and diversity. She is of Filipino heritage and is fluent in the Filipino language. Her study of attachment styles, her deep interest in relationships, and her passion for meaningful work inspire her writing. Michelle works and lives in Southern California with her husband and their much-loved dog.

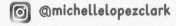 @michellelopezclark    @michellelopezclark    @mlopezclark